*Welsh Woman in London*

# CONTENTS

# CHAPTER 1: A HAPPY CHILDHOOD IN THE WELSH VALLEYS

I wake up in my flat in Camden Town, London. I've lost track of the days. I have no break from my troubled mind. I have nightmares when I'm asleep and crippling depression when I'm awake. I can't leave my flat and can't remember the last time I saw or spoke to anyone. I struggle to breathe with suffocating daily anxiety attacks. Exhausted and unable to take any more, I snap and start raiding my tablet cupboard. Out of the corner of my eye, I catch Dylan, my dog, sitting at my feet looking at me. His beautiful little face and big brown eyes sobers me up. I step back from the cupboard and break into tears of frustration and deep sadness. Desperately wondering when this will stop, and when I will get better. Here is my story of how I got here..

My Name is Ria Davies. I was born In the early 1980's in heart of the Welsh Valleys, amidst rolling hills, and endless greenery. The mountains stood tall like giants overseeing the villages, (in them days) with coal mines scattered throughout the valley. The Miners' strike cast a shadow over the villages, and with it came the closure of the pits, stealing away the livelihood of many. Times were tough, but it was tough for everyone and communities pulled together. Amidst the hardships, there are countless joyful moments that shine brightly in my childhood memories.

I lived in the small village of Cwmbach with my father, mother, older brother, twin brother and our dog 'Lucky' Our house was filled with love and fun. On weekends, my father would take us walking up the steep mountains. I remember my mucky wellies as I struggled to keep up with his long strides. He would point out the different birds and tell us tales of the olden days. He taught me how to make a bow and arrow from fallen branches and how to skim stones across the stream. I remember always feeling the sense of calm and safety in his company.

My father had a nickname - Coco, because he was always smiling. He was a quiet man of simple pleasures - walking the mountains, tinkering in his shed, making moonshine, watching comedy and telling stories that would capture our imaginations. Though he was quiet by nature, his presence filled our home with warmth, laughter and fun.

I was an outgoing, bubbly child, curious about everything and always asked more questions than my brothers. I made friends easily, also comfortably in my own company, spending all my time outdoors playing up the mountain, in the street or on my bike.

At night, My father would watch shows like 'The Old Grey Whistle Test' this was way past our bedtime but my father would tape it on his new VCR which was revolutionary at the time. He would play it back on the telly for my brothers and I on rainy days in, while my mother would be cooking. It was here for the first time we would see the artists we would hear on the radio.

My father indulged our curiosity in music, I remember seeing artists like Stevie Wonder, Sex pistols and David Bowie for the first time and being mesmerised by their looks and talent. "When will I meet people like Stevie?" I asked my father. He smiled and said, "One day, when you're older, you'll travel the world and meet all kinds of people, including people like Stevie." Even then, I remember clearly the travel seed was planted.

As the years passed, change came knocking at our door. My parents decided to part ways, and we all bid farewell to our family home. We moved two miles to a familiar neighbouring village where my extended family from both my mother's and father's sides lived. My no nonsense mother got us settled in no time at our new home in Mountain Ash. I decided I wanted a job so I rang all the salons in the phone book and landed a Saturday job in a salon in Pontypridd.

Then, a year later when I was 14, tragedy struck. One Friday tea time I was on my way out to meet my friends. I walked into the hallway to find my mother with a shocked look on her face holding the phone. She had just hung up from speaking with my uncle. I asked her if she was ok? She told me my father had died of a sudden heart attack on the farm that afternoon. That sentence hit me like a truck. I was shattered, my entire world crashed. As my mother broke the news to my brothers, I sat on the stairs and tried to processed what my mother had just told me, while I listened to her telling my brothers.

The first few teenage years without my father was very hard for me, especially during holiday seasons. The realisation that death is so final, I missed him so much and would often cry when I was alone in my bedroom. At 14 no-one my age really understood, which in all honesty wasn't necessary a bad thing. Although, looking back I remember many of my friend's parents making a special effort to look out for me. Luckily I was outgoing, bubbly, resilient and I got by with these blessings.

Now mid 1990's my brothers and I were now teenagers, my mother had Sky TV installed and MTV lit up the house! Our home echoed with fun, but it was different now – transitioning from childhood giggles to roaring teenage laughter.

My Comprehensive school years were filled with fun times with my friends, skipping school, drinking at the park and laughing until our bellies ached. All we cared about was who had a free house, the rugby club disco and going to Glastonbury and Reading festival. Grunge exploded, Oasis hit the charts, Paul Weller went solo! and I was just about able to get into some pubs.

Meanwhile factories appeared where the coal-mines once stood, Internet arrived in the village library, mobile phones went on sale, the world was changing fast around us. The future was starting to look bright, with opportunities again in the valleys. But I always knew I wanted to travel. At this point I didn't know how, where or when. All I knew was I will be grabbing the first opportunity that comes my way with both hands.

*Mountain Ash*

# CHAPTER 2: TRAVELLED THE WORLD AND 7 SEAS

During my time at my Saturday job at the salon in Pontypridd, I would spend my time sweeping floors and shampooing hair. From the moment I stepped into that salon, I knew I wanted to be a hairdresser. I loved it there. By the time I finished school, I already had a head start on salon experience and could cut and style ladies hair, barber and even do a freehand flat top!

One day, out of the blue, a man I'd never seen before came into the salon and asked me to cut his hair. He claimed to be a friend of my late father's and gave his condolences on my dad's passing a few years prior. As I trimmed his hair, he asked about my career plans after finishing school. When I told him I want a long career as a professional hairdresser, he suggested I look into working on a cruise ship. He said they were always hiring young hairdressers and it would allow me to travel the world, gain experience, get paid and even save. My face lit up and said to him ' I would LOVE to do that!' Before leaving, he scribbled a phone number on a scrap of paper and wrote 'Good luck Ria! Nick' - the contact information was for a company that hired hairdressers for cruise lines 'Steiner' I never saw this man again.

I followed up and called the number, and it led me to a job interview in London with Ian Carmichael, the Queen's personal hairdresser. Ian entered the room, he had such presence. I had never seen anyone like him before, he was one of the sharpest-dressed men I'd ever seen. Beautiful Scottish accent, tall, with a head of gorgeous long blonde corkscrew curls, he looked like he had just stepped off the pages of a magazine. After my interview Ian told me he would be in touch and I returned back to Mountain Ash that evening. A week or two later I received a letter that had the Royal Stamp of approval at the top. Ian hired me! and two months later I was waving goodbye to the Welsh Valleys for their London Academy. After a week of training With Ian I was sent to Liverpool to board a world cruise on a Cunard Cruise ship. I could hardly believe my luck!

I settled in quickly, learned my duties, made friends, and absolutely fell in love with life onboard. Over the next 13 years, I would call many cruise ships home and visit exotic ports of call all across the globe, whilst doing a job I loved. The ocean became my entire world. I had set out to travel and find adventure, and now I was doing it - sailing the seven seas, travelling the world.

I must say working on a cruise ship is an excellent path for career growth and advancement. No matter your background or where you come from, the world truly is your oyster when you work at sea. Cruise lines employ people from all over the world and all walks of life. It's not just a way to see the world for free - it's hard work and requires following strict safety regulations and hotel guidelines. I describe working on a cruise ship as a blend of being in the Navy and working in a luxury hotel. You need discipline, tireless work ethic, and serious people skills to thrive in that environment. Lucky for me, I had all three in spades.

Before long, I excelled at my job, thanks to my friendly valley girl nature I made friends from all over the globe and had plenty of patience when dealing with guests. While I wasn't one for relationships, I did have fun, but nothing serious. I was having the time of my life at sea – working hard, playing hard, succeeding in my career, and always laughing.

During my second contract, I found myself working under a Spa Director who had a significant positive impact on me. Until now sadly I had not met a manager like this. She was respectful, polite, pleasant and genuinely interested in all the staff. Don't get me wrong she wasn't a push over, she was firm, fair and didn't play favourites. Her straightforward approach, especially in dealing with young people, was very effective. She made me recognise in myself a management style that I knew I was capable of adopting. She nurtured my talents, boosting confidence, leading to my further success.

After 3 contracts, I was ready for a new chapter in my career. I now earned a promotion to Spa Director. This role came with officer status and a lot more responsibility. I was in this role for 12 incredible years managing Salons, Spa's, Medi Spa clinics and fitness centres all over the world. Each contract I was assigned to a larger, newer ship, sometimes involving overseeing the launch of a new ship at the shipyard. I worked long hours but the hours didn't seem to matter because I loved my work and ever developing career. When not working, I would enjoy the ship's amenities with my friends, eat at one of the restaurants, watch shows, and explore new destinations during my shore leave.

By my mid-30s, I had circled the globe multiple times over and was starting to think about making some land life plans. This can be quite daunting for those who have spent a long time at sea, the ship becomes your life and family, and adjusting to life ashore can be challenging. It isn't uncommon for people to return back to sea.

By this time, I had become a well-known manager both onboard and in our shoreside office. A new position opened in the Miami corporate office for Sales and Revenue Manager for Royal Caribbean cruises. Ironically reporting to the same Manager who had been my direct report throughout my every role at sea. knowing I thrived under her uncomplicated leadership and the timing aligned perfectly with my plans to settle back on land. I leapt at the opportunity, I got the role and moved to Miami. My knowledge from years working on the ships proved invaluable in this hands on role, leading to a seamless transition.

Within 4 years, I got another promotion, this time to the New Build and Innovation team. As Operation Manager of new Builds and Innovation. I helped plan and outfit brand-new cruise ships from the plans to the steel beams up. It was an amazing experience to see ships brought to life from concept to completion. I worked closely with engineering and interior design teams, coordinated with international shipyards, right up to the delivery launch events around the world and maiden voyage. During this role I would often visit the shipyards in Europe flying via London.

Although I now lived in Miami, my role still kept me travelling globally. Even when oceans apart, I always stayed connected with friends I met at sea, often running into them during my travels. It was safe to say I had a friend in every port and onboard every ship. Back at my home in Miami I kept an open-door policy - anytime someone was passing through they were always welcome.

Throughout my career I often regularly returned home to Wales to spend time with my family and friends. I find visiting my home town extremely grounding and a place where I can sit in the pub and unwind with my family and friends.

In my late 30s, I began to reassess my life in Miami, which came as a shock because my plan had been to stay there. I had established my home, job, and residential visas there, and I had thoroughly enjoyed my time, having lots of fun and forming strong friendships. However, I found myself missing the UK.

Despite 20 years of travels and exposure to different cultures, I remained essentially the same person, even still with my strong Welsh accent. I started to miss British people, humor, and music. Reflecting on my non-stop travel since boarding the ship in Liverpool in November 1999, I realised I had missed many Christmases, Easters, and other special family and friends occasions. Upon reflection, I understood that it was perhaps normal to feel this way.

Also, I had set high expectations for my new life in the Miami office, but the reality was professionally it wasn't what I had expected. It was like looking behind the curtain of the Wizard of Oz. I began considering my options.

Moving back to Mountain Ash seemed boring for a single woman in her late 30's. But the idea of moving to London..Camden Town, London to be more specific made me light up with excitement. There I could still live in a multi cultural environment, satisfy my British cravings, regularly nip home to Wales, and achieve a better work life balance while enjoy the endless music, arts and creativity Camden Town had to offer.

All I needed was a job and new home. I figured with my resume what could go wrong. After careful thought and consideration, weighing up the pros and cons, I resigned from my 20-year career with Steiner. I packed up my home, said goodbye to my friends and moved to London!

# CHAPTER 3: LONDON CALLING

After spending nearly twenty years living the globetrotting lifestyle in the cruise industry, at age 36 I decided it was time to put down some roots back home in the UK. As exciting as my career had been, it was also exhausting to constantly be shipped off to a different country every week. I was ready for a new chapter focused on building a home without relying on immigration visa's.

Although one day my plans are to return to the Valleys or at least have a home there. However at this time being a single woman in my late 30's, I was not ready. A move to London was very appealing to me. As a music fan, Camden Town seemed like the perfect fit with its pubs, culture and constant creative energy.

After packing up my belongings in Miami, I hired a shipping company and bid farewell to all my friends. it was very hard saying goodbye especially to my 2 girlfriends I spent all my free time with. I landed at Heathrow Airport with my plan and a 2 week hotel booking. Ready to build a new life. I felt motivated, optimistic, and adventurous about planting my roots in a new city and finding a career that would allow me to stay in one country for a change.

My global experience in my field and my LinkedIn account gained me a lot of employment prospects. I quickly secured a new role at L'Oreal UK, I was thrilled to be working with such a prestigious company. I secured my new flat in

Cricklewood not far from Camden Town and moved out of my hotel. Within 2 weeks of landing in Heathrow I had checked everything off my list- new job, new home, everything seemed to be falling into place perfectly.

The first few months in London were busy settling in and reconnecting with old friends. Some were from my days working on cruise ships who also now lived in London. I felt so grateful to have made such a big move and for everything to have gone according to plan. Packing up a 20-year life is very daunting, and I felt both thankful and happy.

While reconnecting with old friends, I reconnected with an old acquaintance named 'Chris'. I had first met 'Chris' a few months back during one of my frequent layovers in London on business trips to the shipyard. We got chatting in a hotel bar and exchanged numbers to stay in touch.

'Chris' was very charming—tall, good-looking, funny, and confident. I remembered enjoying his company and having a laugh. Now, reconnecting with him again after a couple of months, he was very happy I had moved to London. He kept telling me how great it was that I was living here now and how we' should spend more time together.

Over the next few weeks, 'Chris' called and texted me quite frequently, wanting to meet up, take walks on Hampstead Heath, go for food, or just come over and watch a film. He quickly made it clear that his intentions were romantic, not just friendly.

At first, I brushed off his advances, mainly because he had told me he was in his late 20s and I was 36 at this point. Although the age gap was not too noticeable as he was very mature, it felt a bit too large of an age difference for a serious relationship in my opinion. But 'Chris' persisted, telling me not to worry about the age difference. He said he had always been drawn to older, mature women and didn't care at all that I was older.

While I remained hesitant about pursuing a relationship with a younger man, I had to admit that I thoroughly enjoyed Chris's company. He was charming, funny, and seemed genuinely interested in getting to know me better. We had great conversations and were always laughing.

In this world of milk and honey, my priority in life has always been my career. I was settling in great at L'Oreal, and enjoying ever minute of it, working with lovely people. Not taking Chris too seriously, I agreed to see how things would go. Over the next few weeks, he would text me daily, stay at my flat, regularly confess that he had growing feelings for me, and remind me that he wanted to pursue a serious relationship. He constantly told me I was beautiful and intelligent and that he had never clicked with anyone the way he did with me. It was like I was the centre of his world.

Then one day, we went for Sunday lunch at a pub in Hampstead. It started subtly, but he began to accuse me of checking out other men. I thought he was joking. I found the accusation bizarre and laughed it off, lightly telling him not to be silly.

Then, shortly after, while driving home, he was very quiet in the car. Out of nowhere, he punched me full force in the face while I was driving around a roundabout in Chalk Farm. My head slammed against the window, and I lost control of the steering wheel. Quickly regaining control of the car, I registered what he had just done. I was stunned. He said to me in a cold voice, "Stop checking out the men on the pavement, you fucking slut." It was clear he had just shown me a side of himself that was dark and ugly.

I pulled over and told him to get out of the car, He lived around the corner and he did just that. From that point on, I kept my distance from him. I wrote him off as a young man with issues he needed to sort out. I told myself to forget what happened, to move on, and to continue building my new life in London. And that's exactly what I did.

Moving to London couldn't have gone smoother. However, in the next chapter, you will see my story take a turn. My world became a living nightmare. Little did I know this charming, good-looking, charismatic man was a violent predator, and like all predators, they hide in plain sight and silence their victims with embarrassment and shame, wearing your soul down so much that you don't recognise yourself.

Using a variety of psychological techniques to gain control of their victims, which experts refer to as **"the wheel of abuse,"** they manipulate, dominate, and poison every part of your life.

# CHAPTER 4: THE WHEEL OF ABUSE

L ife at L'Oréal was going great. I was meeting new and interesting people and thoroughly enjoying it. After working 20 years at my previous company, I was incredibly relieved that this was the case.

As the weeks went on Chris would contact me over text to profoundly apologise and share his embarrassment about the incident in the car. He shared that he had jealousy and anger issues. A few weeks later, he started to ask me to meet up with him so he could apologise to my face.

After a few weeks, as friends, I agreed to go to the mall where he continued to express remorse over his actions.

I told him I accepted his apology and shared that he would end up in serious trouble one day if he continued behaving like this, and that he should seek help ASAP.

He agreed and asked me to help him research therapists and if we could do it together at my flat. Though reluctant, I wanted to support his efforts to get help. After all, he wasn't the first troubled soul I had helped in my time, so I agreed.

Back at my flat I was cooking dinner when I realised I didn't have a tin opener. I suggested I would knock on my neighbour's door to ask if I could borrow one. Chris waited in my doorway watching me as I knocked my neighbour's door. My neighbour kindly invited me in and he handed me a tin opener. When I returned, Chris was no longer waiting in the doorway. As I entered my flat, he was sitting inside, across the room. He abruptly stood up and charged at me, punching me in the face. I was knocked off my feet and fell hard to the floor. He jumped on top of me, grabbing my throat and strangling me until I lost consciousness.

When I regained consciousness, he was throwing water in my face to revive me.

What followed was days of vicious assaults that left me bloodied, bruised, and traumatised. He told me over and over that I deserved this violence for going into another man's home. In between violent episodes, he continued berating me emotionally, calling me a Welsh whore and a Welsh slag. He took my phone to see which men were in my call history. Holding me by the hair, he forced me to call each male contact back while he listened on speakerphone. When my twin brother's name came up, he refused to believe it was my brother, violently shaking my head and spitting in my face as he demanded I tell the truth.

Whilst I was asleep he opened my laptop and permanently deleted my Facebook account that I had for 13 years. I was distraught about losing 13 years of my world travel photos and memories. Even worse, the childhood pictures of my dearest late father. I could see he was enjoying the upset this caused me.

Chris told me that if I dared tell anyone what happened, no one would believe me. In his words, they would finally see me for the weak, pathetic old woman I was. He constantly berated me as depressing, and worthless, underscoring how I had no friends or family who cared enough to visit me.

Everything I celebrated about myself, being independent, relying on no-one in this case became my downfall. No one was checking on me. It wasn't unusual if I didn't make contact for a few day or even weeks. I wasn't missed. His message was clear: I was completely alone.

Then, a few days later, out of the blue, a close childhood friend called to say she was in London and wanted to visit me at my new flat. As soon as I hung up the phone, I told Chris my friend would be arriving shortly. He quickly gathered his things, told me he would text me later, and left. I was so relieved but still in a state of shock. I hid my injuries as best I could, though inside I was traumatised. My friend arrived, and we went to the pub. I was so happy to see her.

At the end of the night, my friend opened the bathroom door while I was inside and saw my bruises. She was horrified and wanted to know what happened. I told her everything, reassured her I had it under control, and made her swear to secrecy. I was still in shock and didn't want to worry anyone; I was embarrassed. She couldn't believe someone had done this to me, but she kept her promise not to tell and was burdened with the worry. To this day, I feel terrible for worrying my friend like this.

Over the next few weeks, Chris would disappear, and I wouldn't hear from him for days, only for him to reappear demanding to see me. He would send apologetic texts, expressing his concern for me and apologising for what he did. He would notice my car wasn't outside and ask where I was. I made excuses, saying I was working to avoid him, all while noticing my mood deteriorating. I told no one, trying to keep up appearances. Once the weekend came, I would sometimes go out but mostly I would spend my days in bed watching films.

I decided the only way to protect myself was to move. A month later, after Christmas. I relocated to West Hampstead, with the aim to forget what happened and put it behind me.

# CHAPTER 5: BREAKING POINT

My new home in West Hampstead was lovely. The street had great shops and bars, and the transport links were the best in London. I joined a guitar class and made a lovely friend there. Work was going great, and spring had arrived. I love Spring, it gives me the feeling of lots to look forwards to.

Then a phone call came out of the blue. It was May 22nd, 2018 and I was just finishing for the day when my phone rang with an unknown number. I hesitated before answering, but something told me to pick up.

It was Chris calling me from an unfamiliar number. He told me he was in the hospital, having an unexpected operation on his hand. He said he had been kicked out of his flat and had nothing - no clothes, no toiletries. He asked if I could please bring him some things to get by before he goes down to theatre.

I was caught off guard and wary, considering our tumultuous history. He heard the hesitation in my silence and he quickly apologised for how he had treated me, saying he was ashamed of what he did and shared that I was the nicest woman he had ever met and misses me a great deal. He told me he had no-one else to call and added that he was now getting help to manage his anger issues. He seemed sincere in his request. Feeling sorry for him and giving him the benefit of the doubt, I agreed to visit him at the hospital.

I brought some new pajamas, his favorite snacks, and toiletries. When I arrived, he was so happy to see me. He asked for a "cwtch," which is Welsh for a hug. He whispered in my ear, "Thank you for coming, and I'm so sorry for what I did." He started to tear up and get emotional. To comfort him, I told him not to worry about that now and to tell me what happened. He told me he fell off his motorbike.

Shortly after, the doctor came to let him know he would be taken down shortly for his operation. Chris turned to me, and in a panicked tone of voice, asked if I could please be there when he came out of the theater. I told him yes.

I stayed with him when he returned from the theater until he came around. As he slowly regained consciousness, he smiled, reached for my hand, and thanked me for being there.

The next day I got a text from him thanking me for being there and asking to bring him some other bits. I agreed and told him I would pass by the hospital after work.

That evening I visited, he was back to the charismatic, funny person I had met. We laughed together like old friends. He was kept in for a few more days, which he resented, so I visited him after work to keep him company. Those days almost made me forget the darker times.

When it came time for him to be discharged, he called me again. He asked if he could come to my flat for a few hours while waiting for the keys to his new flat. I was hesitant—he didn't know where I lived now, or what new car I was driving and I wanted to keep it that way.

However, he addressed the elephant in the room and my concerns head-on, saying he understood but assuring me he had changed. He pointed to our pleasant days together in the hospital as proof, along with the therapy he had been receiving for anger management. And added after being there for him at the hospital he wouldn't dare suggest this if he was not in a better place with all his issues. Reluctantly, I agreed to let him stay for a short while.

I collected him after work from the hospital and brought him to my flat. He was in my flat for an hour, his demeanour shifted. He was constantly on his phone, tense and irritable. As I walked past him, I caught a glimpse of his screen. He saw me look. It was open to a dating app called Grindr. In a flash of rage, he leapt up and punched me in the face with his casted hand. My mouth exploded in blood.

He tore all my clothes off, leaving me naked and unable to run for help. Then he wrapped his hands around my throat, choking the life out of me. As my vision darkened, the last thing I saw was the pure hatred in his eyes, the look of a killer.

I came to with him throwing water in my face. In shock, I jumped up and tried to run to the door. He stabbed my leg with a long cooker lighter, causing me to collapse to the floor

He kicked and stomped all over my legs relentlessly so I couldn't walk. Then he dragged my bloodied, half-conscious body by the hair into the bathroom and threw me into the empty bath tub.

Laying there, barely conscious, beaten to my near death I truly thought he was going to kill me. But instead, he just laughed, and started to take photos of me, and threatened to send them to my family and friends if I told anyone what happened. He said he would post the pictures of me online and because I work for L'Oreal he threatened to post a copy of the pictures in every salon letterbox in London.

Finally, after what I felt was hours. He pulled me out from the bath tub and carried me to my bed, giving me paracetamol and sleeping pills. He wouldn't let me put on any clothes on. He placed the chair by the door so I couldn't leave and continued on his phone. He held me captive for three more days, continuously beating and degrading me. He kept punching my legs so I couldn't walk. He was bending my fingers, grabbing my face and pushing my cheeks in. He was shoving and punching my head. He also kept kicking my body, standing on my legs and spitting at me. I was his prisoner, subjected to evil violent assaults, unimaginable cruelty and wicked verbal attacks. He kept calling me a "Welsh slut" and to "f*ck off back to Wales or to Miami." He repeatedly told me he was going to throw acid on me, called me old, depressing, dirty and boring. He kept saying how ugly I was and no wonder I was not married and had no children.

When I woke on the third day, to my suprise he was gone. I quickly locked the door behind him, got dressed, called a taxi, and went straight to A&E. I was in shock, deeply ashamed and embarrassed about what had happened. So I told them at the desk I fell off my bike. I was seen right away.

Some parts of my body had clear hand prints and teeth marks so during a brief examination the nurse confronted me about my injuries. I broke down, telling her everything.

When the Doctor arrived he asked if I could get undressed for a closer examination. As I took my clothes off, he saw the extent of my battered body. I heard the nurse gasp and the doctor's face fell. He stepped out of the room and later returned with the police. He explained whoever did this would end up killing me if he wasn't stopped. They took my statement, even as I said I didn't want to press charges. I was crying and rambling on saying I just wanted it all to go away and I want to go home. Not wanting to push me too far they got me to agree to see a domestic violence advocate. Which I agreed.

When I returned to my flat, I cleaned the blood off the walls, changed my bloody bed sheets, and scrubbed the blood out of the bathroom tiles. I collected the hair that had been pulled out from the roots, threw out the clothes he had torn off me, straightened the furniture, and went to sleep.

After this incident I was struggling to hold myself together.

After the hospital referral, I had finally managed to register with a GP after being refused by multiple practices that claimed they were full.

Shortly after registering, I received a call from a domestic violence advocate who wanted to meet me at a cafe in Camden Town. I nervously agreed.

We met at the cafe and I opened up to her about everything that had happened. But throughout our conversation, she seemed distracted, constantly checking her phone. Abruptly, she said she had to leave and would follow up with me later. I never heard from her again.

Her dismissive behaviour left me paranoid. I wondered if she was even who she claimed to be. I started to get even more paranoid thinking did she know Chris? My trust in getting help from professionals was diminishing.

Outwardly, I carried on as normal, throwing myself into my work. But inside, my mental health was in rapid decline. The assaults I had endured kept replaying in vivid detail in my mind. I started to experience panic attacks and nightmares.

The following week I had to go into the office for a regional work meeting. with the rest of our team. I was still in physical pain, with bruises on my body. I hide them with dark stockings and long sleeves. I told my coworkers I had fallen off a bike to excuse my mobility.

My depression and anxiety were worsening, so I finally went to see my new GP. When he reviewed my file, he saw my recent visits to A&E after the attacks. The doctor told me I am suffering from PTSD, prescribed anti-depressants and encouraged me to be referred to 'Safety Net' a domestic violence organisation in Camden.

I told him about the woman who I had met in Camden Town and she had brushed me off. He seemed just as puzzled by her behaviour. But he assured me the local Camden Safety Net advocates would follow up with me and provide real help.

The next day, I received a call from my new advocate. She was originally from Northern England but now lived in London. Her friendly, patient demeanour immediately put me at ease.

She educated me about the dynamics of domestic violence. She said it was common for trauma and NDE survivors to experience PTSD symptoms like mine when living in constant "fight or flight" mode. She likened healing to gradually thawing after being frozen and assured me I would start to understand and make sense of what had happened.

The advocate explained the "cycle of abuse"—how manipulative abusers use a repeating pattern of loving behaviour and violence to control their victims. Explained the manipulation tactics that result in victims forgiving the perpetrator, even worse depending on their perpetrator, and how they shame victims into silence. This all made sense to me.

I continued meeting with the advocate over the next few weeks. I had no experience to draw from and she helped me with knowledge of my situation. For the first time, I felt hopeful.

Meanwhile, Chris started calling and texting me frequently from yet another new number asking to see me. In his texts he was sharing that he was concerned about me. That he was sorry. That he missed me. I ignored his attempts to contact me, wanting nothing more than to move on with my life.

I was disappointed in myself for knowing this man let alone trusting him. But thanks to my advocate, I was beginning to understand I was not to blame. The shame and embarrassment I had felt was shifting into understanding my situation.

Eventually, Chris seemed to realise that his apologies and promises would no longer manipulate me. So he switched tactics once again, resorting to threats to embarrass and control me.

He had previously threatened to throw acid on my face—a vain attempt at intimidation. Since I'm not a particularly vain woman he stopped threating me with Acid and switched to a campaign of hate and humiliation.

As punishment for ignoring him, Chris set up online fake lesbian dating profiles, prostitute profiles and naked massage services.

He included my name, photos, address and contact details. I was bombarded with calls through the day and night with propositions from strangers. Men even showed up at my home.

When I walked to my car in the mornings, I would find it vandalized with words "Welsh slag" smeared in ketchup.

The abuser sent intimate videos of himself with other women, texting me that she is better than me—a desperate grasp at provoking a reaction from me.

Then he threatened to print the photos of me he took in the bath and post them in every hair salon in London. He wanted me to know he could destroy my reputation at any time. I snapped and called him back. He would answer and hang up enjoying that he's now got a reaction out of me.

The mind games, harassment, and public shaming attempts made me constantly anxious and afraid. The abuser was proving he had zero limits and I'd lost all control over what he might do next.

Late one Sunday night, after another weekend of over 300 calls, I received a call from a coworker checking in on me about our meeting the next day. Ironically I did mention to him early that month I was having issues with an old acquaintance.

I was so worn down. He could tell something was wrong and asked me if I was ok. I broke down and told him more details about everything that was happening. He was older, worldly and we had a great working relationship.

He calmly but strongly urged me to call HR at work and disclose the abuse. He reassured me that our HR manager was excellent and she would help me.

Earlier that week, when my phone wouldn't stop ringing at work, I confessed to another trusted coworker, whom I always found to be a lovely, thoughtful, and genuine person. She was in the meeting that day when I told everyone I had fallen off a bike. She was understanding and supportive, helping me feel less alone and not embarrassed. Her friendship continues to be a source of strength to this day. Drawing strength from these two supportive experiences at work, I decided to take my colleague's advice and call HR.

The next morning, I phoned HR and told her about the months of abuse I had endured. She was shocked at the horrific violence I had been subjected to. She listened patiently and empathetically, assuring me that everything would be okay.

I explained how I was experiencing repeated night terrors, anxiety attacks, and deepening depression. I was nervous to go online and even to go to my car.

She advised me to take the day off, make an appointment with my doctor, and said she would check on me later. She told me not to worry about my schedule and that she would speak to my manager. She reassured me that I had the company's full support.

I went to my Doctor that day and was prescribed a higher dose of antidepressants. He diagnosing me with PTSD and signed me off for 2 months. When I returned home, I found flowers at my door from HR with a note reassuring me that everything was going to be okay. It was such a lovely gesture it made me smile. Exhausted I went to bed and didn't leave my flat for 2 weeks.

My low mood and nightmares was terrible but sharing what was happening with my 2 compassionate coworkers and my domestic violence advocate had shown me some support.

Being in my flat became increasingly unbearable. To me, it was now "the house of horrors." I was still finding streaks of my blood staining the walls, and the memories of how I nearly lost my life there were traumatic. The thought of Chris knowing where I lived left me feeling constantly on edge.

My counsellor from Camden Safety Net helped me move into a new flat where no-one knew where I was. It was a cute little studio on a council estate in Chalk Farm. It had a great big security gate, giving a small community feel. The flat was newly refurbished, and I was 3rd on the offer list.

The day I visited the flat, Viewer number 1 didn't show up. I was waiting with Viewer number 2, an Irish lady who had just been released from prison. We stood in the courtyard as the housing officer walked toward us. The Irish lady (Viewer number 2) looked up at the other floors, then turned to me and said, "Nah, this ain't the place for me. The flat's all yours." She looked at the housing officer and said whilst pointing at me, "She's got the flat, right?" Then she tapped me on the back and walked off. And just like that I was viewer number 1 and got my new home.

I collected the keys that week. The flat was fitted with CCTV, I moved in the following week and quickly got settled in. Shortly after I went back to work and carried on with my life aiming to put the whole awful 18 months behind me.

# CHAPTER 6: NEGLIGENT PEOPLE IN POWER

After the brutal attack, I quickly settled into my new flat and went back to work. My plan was to forget about what happened and move on with my life. However, I greatly underestimated the lingering effects of such a traumatic experience.

On top of dealing with the aftermath, my new neighbourhood was not what it seemed. Sending me and all my underlying problems down a dangerous road.

My new studio flat was in a local council estate. I was born on a council estate. Knowing I would fit in anywhere I was excited to become part of a community. It was a fresh start in a beautiful new home, and I dove back into my job, determined to get my life back on track.

I made it my focus to keep my thoughts centred on what originally brought me to London - Music, culture, and the excitement of city living. I treated the attacks as a "rough patch" I acknowledged that, understandably, this experience would affect me, but I truly believed I would soon return to my normal self.

Like I've always done in new cities, with the aim of making new friends. I joined a gym, I started popping into the local pubs. I soon met a local man named Terry who became my regular pub pal. Terry was the quintessential pub friend - easy to talk to, knew everyone, and was always up for going for a pint. I finally got myself a dog and named him Dylan after Bob Dylan. Dylan immediately became my BFF and spent all our time together exploring the neighbourhood.

During our walks to the dog park, I met a friendly young mother. She was outgoing and ambitious, and we quickly and easily became friends. I finally felt like I was starting to put down roots and things were taking shape just like they had in Miami.

But the periods of depression I experienced after the attacks grew increasingly dark and more frequent. Eventually, I opened up to Terry and my other local friend about what happened. They were both incredibly supportive. Terry didn't seem surprised and explained that controlling, abusive behaviour was something he'd unfortunately seen many times before. My other local friend, wise beyond her years, was deeply understanding, non-judgemental, like the ultimate wing woman.

Meanwhile, a new problem started arising. The constant noise and antisocial behaviour around my ground floor flat grew harder to tolerate over time. Kids kicked footballs outside my door from dawn till dusk against the giant iron gate. Teenagers hung out on the steps daily, which was mostly just a nuisance. Upstairs, grown women carried on loud conversations and spiteful innuendos targeting their latest prey. Their adult bullying and name-calling were shocking. But worst of all was the constant thudding of the footballs against the metal gate outside my window, was triggering my PTSD.

I decided to speak to the housing officer in charge of the estate since his office was onsite, only about 10 meters from my back window. He casually told me to just fill out a log, which struck me as odd—not only could he probably hear the thudding from his office, but I also asked why he couldn't simply walk the estate himself to witness the problem and address it on the spot. It's just a bunch of kids who need to be directed to the football area in the next street. Job done. I could have done it myself, but as a resident, it's simply not my place. I added there's no way I am the only one being disturbed by this. He didn't have a response; he just stood there with his mouth open.

Nevertheless, I followed his instructions and filled out the log. When I followed up on the action plan, he said he had lost the log paper. His response bowled me over. It was a small office with just a few drawers. How could he be so careless as to lose a piece of paper I had handed him? and where on earth did he lose the paper?

My mental health started deteriorating. The periods of depression became more frequent, the nightmares about the attacks grew vivid, and my overall behaviour changed.

The noise surrounding my flat was like gasoline on a fire. I ditched the log and started documenting my disputes in writing. I continued emailing the housing officer, but all I received was lip service, as he remained dismissive and negligent. At one point he told me the previous resident had happily lived in my flat for 25 years, implying the problem was me.

I later learned that she had allegedly been harassed extensively by ASB, suffered from mental illness, and had no family. One day, she allegedly snapped, set herself and the flat on fire, was airlifted to the hospital, and later died there. I googled it and was horrified to read about her story online. What shocked me even more was realising that my housing officer was fully aware of this, yet had the audacity to pretend otherwise and still remains a charlatan of a manager.

I followed the council's handbook, persistently reporting the antisocial behaviour and holding my housing officer accountable for following each outlined step. But I saw no change, no improvement, despite my diligent efforts and follow up.

He wouldn't even walk the grounds of his work place without a police officer with him. After much back and forth, and constant follow up, the housing officer finally came to me with some action. He arranged a meeting for me to speak with the local Labour councillor. I was so pleased—I had never met, let alone needed to speak to, an elected official before, and I assumed she would take my situation seriously.

I emailed her a summary ahead of our meeting, copying the housing officer, explaining precisely why I was requesting her help and how I'd come to live in this flat. Attaching a letter from Camden Safety Net. She responded confirming the appointment. That Saturday morning I went to her at her Surgery.

As a resident I was paying towards a security service. Therefore, there was already a system in place. It just needed to be followed up and flagged by community leaders.

The outcome I was expecting, was that after explaining the situation, she would understand how impossible it was to live like this. Recognise the lethargic management style of my housing office, take control of the situation and use the tools available to resolve the antisocial behaviour around my flat.

Instead, looking at me over her glasses in a condescending manner, she proceeded to slowly draw a map of my building on a piece of paper. She highlighted areas "notorious" for antisocial behaviour as if I was unaware. She went on and suggested that after work I should go to the cinema to avoid the noise at home.

As if this related to my situation, she offhandedly mentioned being disturbed herself on occasion by noise from Hampstead Heath near her own home.

She capped it off by stating that London is a busy city, not a small village community like in the Welsh valleys, implying I was some country bumpkin unaccustomed to city living.

I was shocked by her dismissive, snobby, and negligent attitude—after all, she was an elected Labour councillor supposed to represent the people.

This smiling, supposedly caring Labour councillor, whose profile was splashed across local papers and the internet, giving the impression of a caring, proactive woman in action, was nothing of the sort.

She was so out of touch, snobby, condescending and clearly didn't care or plan to help me address the serious and illegal issues I had brought to her attention. It baffled me how she was in such an important position.

I reported significant antisocial behaviour problems, illegal activity, and safety concerns, and she suggested I go see a film after work while insulting my Welsh roots. Little did she know I was a world-travelled seaman who had visited some of the most dangerous places on this planet.

Our meeting concluded with her asking me to email suggestions on how she could address my situation, which was surprising since she was fully aware of the hotspots, as she clearly noted on the map she drew with her crayons. Back home, I immediately emailed her a detailed list of reasonable, actionable steps.

Six long weeks later, having received no reply, I followed up. Her response was that she does not deal with antisocial behaviour issues. This begged the question - Then why on earth did my housing officer set up this meeting? and why did she herself agree to meet with me?

It was a complete waste of time. This Labour representative, who has been elected by the public is responsible for solving complex community issues that vulnerable people rely on.

I felt deeply let down by the safeguarding measures, which failed me on every level. Instead of receiving support, I was met with snobbery, ignorance, and negligence. This shattered my trust in both her and the entire system.

Feeling hopeless, with a negligent housing officer, a useless meeting with a Labour official, and the antisocial behaviour growing even worse, the Covid lockdown then began.

One morning early in lockdown, a heroin user opened my window and tried to climb into my flat. Thankfully my dog

Dylan started barking and lunged at the man and he ran off. The public drug use and dealing outside my back window increased severely, leaving me with the attitude 'Oh look there's someone smoking crack or injecting heroin again'.

A few weeks into lockdown, my mental health took a steep decline. I knew that had nothing to do with lockdown. I was accustomed to spending weeks alone while traveling by myself for years. I was furloughed from work and my days were filled with anti social behaviour all around my ground floor flat. My flat was a studio and I couldn't escape it. The periods of depression became more frequent.. Unlike myself, I began to cry constantly and experienced vivid, terrifying flashbacks of the attacks when I was awake.

When asleep, vivid nightmares of Chris played like a horror movie, over and over in my mind. When awake, I started to hear his voice making abusive remarks and see dark shadows moving around the room.

My racing thoughts of the attacks prevented me from sleeping for days on end. I'd finally crash into a deep, almost comatose sleep, losing all track of time and days. Whether awake or asleep, I now had no rest from the torment in my mind. I desperately wanted it to stop. As a result, to my shock I started experiencing strong, impulsive suicidal thoughts.

My caring local friend grew worried when she hadn't heard from me for a few days. My phone was filled with missed calls and messages. She came by my flat and immediately saw I was unwell. She reassured me this was a normal reaction given everything that had happened to me and all the ongoing ASB around my flat. She encouraged me to call the urgent NHS helpline.

I could no longer pretend I was fine. It didn't matter how much I wanted to put what had happened behind me; I couldn't escape my own mind. My mental health had completely consumed me, and I was experiencing my first nervous breakdown.

# CHAPTER 7: MENTAL HEALTH CRISIS

The months leading up to my mental health crisis were among the darkest and most frightening. The assaults, manipulation, online stalking, and embarrassment, coupled with the fact that my new home was the epicenter of ASB, crime, and drugs, combined with the incompetence of those in charge and my own struggle to keep everything under control, all came to a head. My mind had completely consumed me, and I was experiencing my first nervous breakdown.

When COVID-19 hit and the country went into lockdown, things only got worse. With nowhere to escape to, I was trapped in my flat day and night, subjected to constant noise, footballs, and addicts. The mental abuse from Chris rang fresh in my mind, as he often told me things like "no one cares about you" and "no one even calls to check on you." At this point, those words felt truer than ever.

In reality, people never checked on me because they weren't used to doing so. I was always traveling, in a different time zone, on a flight, or at sea. Friends and family would simply wait until I phoned or showed up, as I always eventually did. Never in their wildest dreams could they have imagined what I was really going through.

I barely slept, plagued by graphic nightmares where Chris would torture and try to kill me. During the day, I was overwhelmed by anxiety and depression, sometimes becoming hysterical with tears for no reason. I started "hearing voices" and seeing things that weren't there – later I'd learned this was due to lack of sleep resulting in extreme exaustion. I would try to keep calm, telling myself it was not real and cwtch my dog.

One morning, after another sleepless night, I completely broke down. The mental anguish had become unbearable. Sobbing uncontrollably, I called the 24-hour mental health crisis line that my domestic violence worker had given me. Within an hour, a mental health crisis team was at my door to evaluate me.

I was nearly incoherent, rambling about the constant drug use outside my window, the relentless banging of footballs, and how the authorities—who are supposed to address these issues—shamelessly ignored my complaints. I also spoke of the vivid nightmares that left me terrified to sleep. The team listened patiently, taking notes. After about half hour, they calmly suggested that, for my own safety and further evaluation, it would be best if I came into the overnight psychiatric crisis centre.

This was sobering and I was very frightened. I even began to wonder if I was being tricked into a padded cell. Lately, nothing and nobody seemed as they should. I felt surrounded by liars and bad people I couldn't trust.

My local friend came over and agreed that it was a good idea I went there even if it was for some respite. She offered to look after my dog and assured me she would take good care of him.

I gathered a small bag of belongings, locked up my flat, and headed to St. Pancras Hospital.

When I arrived, I was shown to my plain yet comfortable room, which had a single bed, a window, and an ensuite bathroom.

I was evaluated by the doctor and psychiatrist, who diagnosed me with C-PTSD. They explained that this is a mental health condition resulting from a traumatic experience, and in my case, a near-death experience (NDE). They reviewed my medications, and increased the dose.

After my evaluation, I went to my room and slept until the next day. The building resembled a ward, but each patient had their own room. The other patients had a range of mental health conditions, such as psychosis, schizophrenia, and depression. One man mentioned that he to had PTSD.

After getting settled, I had a meeting with the crisis centre manager. She exuded a calm, caring energy. She sat with me and asked me to tell her what happened and start from where I see fit. I told her everything I'd been dealing with over the past 2 years. The brutal assaults from Chris, how I moved on to a new home, the failures of the housing officer in charge of my building. The incident with the Labour Councillor.

She listened attentively, her expression serious but kind. She didn't judge or interrupt me. When I finished, she said, "There is no wonder you are here." She thanked me for sharing everything and reassured me that I was now in a safe place and I was going to be OK.

Over the next couple of days the new dose of medication started to kick in. The rooms were designed to prevent any attempts at suicide: there were no coat hangers, and the shower sprayed directly from the wall. There were occasions when patients would start to argue with one another but it got shut down quickly. The staff were very much in control and the building was clearly well run. I felt safe there, a feeling I hadn't experienced in a long time.

The days had a comforting routine. In the morning medication was taken under supervision, followed by breakfast. We ate all our meals together at the dining table in the recreation area. The staff were available 24/7 incase of emergencies. Lights out was at 10 p.m., and they would check on you throughout the night through your window.

In our free time, we could watch TV, read, or go into the garden area, while keeping within the social distancing rules. I spent my days playing ping pong with other patients and sweeping up leaves in the garden. Throughout the day, the mental health staff and the manager would sporadically check in with us, and they all proved to be an invaluable support.

My thoughtful friend would send me lovely videos of my dog Dylan out on walks and playing. These never failed to make me smile and brought me great comfort.

Meanwhile, my local friend Terry noticed he hadn't heard from me in a couple of days and that I wasn't picking up my messages. He texted to check if I was okay. I told him where I was and what had happened. Terry, someone I can always count on, visited me during visiting hours that day.

About a week into my stay, one of the mental health nurses suggested we take a walk together on the hospital grounds. As we strolled, she asked, "Ria, did you press charges with the police for the stalking and attacks?"

I told her no and explained that I felt the police would probably think I deserved it for letting him back into my life after the first incident in the car. I also told her about my life before I came to London and expressed how I felt I had let myself down by allowing someone so dangerous and cruel into my life. I spoke about how ashamed and embarrassed I would feel if my family and friends knew what I had gotten myself into.

I also shared my thoughts on, 'What if it's me?' I mean, he wasn't always like this—we got along very well. What if he's right? What if I really am a miserable woman who made him do these things?

She asked me if I was aware of **the wheel of abuse**? and all the tactics it involved? She explained **this is what keeps people in abusive relationships,** resulting in victims thinking the way I just explained.

She went on and explained that the abuser firstly love bombs their victims, then typically isolates them, after the assaults, they shower them with affection and apologies. This emotional rollercoaster creates a trauma bond and shame making it extremely difficult for the victim to leave.

She went on to tell me about more tactics and pointed out that the rinse and repeat of these tactics will wear anyone's soul down, resulting in you question yourself. Tactics such as gaslighting, coercive control, and narcissistic personality—terms I had never heard before.

Finally, she asked if I was familiar with **Clare's Law,** which I wasn't. She encouraged me to read up on it and apply, suggesting that Clare's Law might help clear away any lingering doubts and self-blame. Which will be key to my recovery and moving forwards.

The next week passed and it was nearly time for my discharge. Along with my care plan and new medication, the staff submitted reports to the relevant authorities about my dangerous housing environment and its negligent management.

The days leading up to my discharge were filled with dread. I had made progress in understanding and processing what had happened to me, thanks to the compassionate staff who took the time to listen and explain things clearly. However, the thought of returning to my flat filled me with dread. Despite my anxiety about leaving, I couldn't wait to see Dylan so I just focused on this.

Just before I was due to leave, I received a call on my mobile from a number I didn't recognise. It was Chris. He spoke quietly and told me he knew I had been in the hospital. He also knew where I lived. He said he was very sorry I was unwell and that he knew it was because of what he had done to me.

He said he wanted to make amends by being there for me when I returned home. Chris mentioned that he thinks about me all the time and is currently in treatment for anger management. He also expressed concern about where I was living, noting that it's a notoriously dangerous building and neighborhood.

I was instantly suspicious as to why he got in touch. But I was exhausted mentally and physically, and the thought of dealing with the antisocial behaviour around my flat made the devil I knew seem a better option than the ones I didn't. Against my better judgment, I agreed he could meet me at my flat once I had settled in.

Chris arrived shortly after I got home. He gave me a big hug and told me how much he's missed me, adding that he's been worried sick about me. At first, he was helpful, and attentive, doing all he could to assist me. But after a couple of days, the buzzer to my flat went off. There were around 70 flats in my building and you could see from my window who was buzzing at the main gate. I looked out and saw it was one of my neighbours trying to get into the building.

In a flash, Chris flew into a rage, accusing me of having a relationship with this man and being unfaithful to him. I tried to explain that it was perfectly normal for neighbours to occasionally buzz the wrong flat by accident, but he called me a 'lying Welsh slag' and punched me hard in the side of my face, knocking me unconscious.

I woke up where I had landed in the hallway, overwhelmed by blinding pain in my head. My vision was blurry. He dragged me to my feet by my hair and proceeded to assault me—biting my face and arms, kicking me, throwing me against the wall, and shoving my cheeks into my face.

He eventually stopped and left me in the bathroom, bleeding, sore, and struggling to see. I told him I needed an ambulance. To my surprise, he agreed but asked what I was going to tell the operator about what happened. I told him I would say I fell off a bike. Satisfied with my answer, he allowed me to call 999, but only if I put the call on speakerphone so he could monitor what I said.

The operator advised me to go straight to A&E. As soon as I hung up, Chris snatched my phone, threw it across the room, and began trashing my flat. When he was done destroying everything, he left.

In agony and blurry vision, I walked a mile to the hospital. This time, **I was ready.** I told the doctors what had happened to me and they called the police. A statement was taken, I returned home the police fitted an emergency response blue box, extra CCTV was fitted and my address was priory marked for 999 calls.

I was contacted by a separate police man, he came to my house, took my statement and said he would be in touch once he has arrested Chris.

After I reported everything to the police, detailing where I was living, I lived alone, how I ended up there, and my recent breakdown, the community police began making regular visits to my house to check on me. This didn't go unnoticed by my neighbours, which seemed to provoke some spiteful behaviour toward me, and the neighbours above escalated their antisocial behaviour to a new level.

One morning a few days later, I was cleaning my windows outside, with my earphones in and another neighbour approached me. She was clearly drunk and told me the women shouting from the upper floors were deliberately targeting me, and that I should watch my back.

It was like she was trying to get a rise out of me. I never have had time for this kind of talk so I thanked her for the heads up, wished her a nice day and put my earphones back in.

I could feel my other neighbours watching from their balconies, as if they were waiting to see how I would react to this interaction.

I was fully aware of the women she was referring to but I wasn't completely sure what they looked like, as they never addressed me directly, only shouted from their balconies 3 floors above.

It turned out the ring leader was a woman in her 50s who had passed me many times in the courtyard. The two other ladies in their 40's struck up a friendly conversations with me many times.

I dismissed the hostility from a group of unpleasant women, figuring I had enough going on. However, other neighbours informed me that they were spreading rumours around the estate that I had CCTV because I was a pedophile. I was sick to my stomach that grown women would knowingly make such dangerous false accusation.

Given what I had already experienced on this estate, I wasn't entirely surprised by their spiteful behaviour.

I remember thinking about what had allegedly happened to the woman who lived in my flat before me. Experiencing life there firsthand, I had no doubt that what I'd heard was probably true.

Shortly I moved to a new address.

# CHAPTER 8: LAW AND ORDER

After uncovering Chris's violent history through 'Claire's Law,' I brought him to justice. However, does justice truly mean justice for victims? I couldn't start trauma therapy until after the trial since his lawyer could claim that the treatment altered my memories of events. So I was placed on high medication doses to stay safe, drastically changing my appearance with extreme weight gain.

I moved into my new home and I was over the moon. After the last place I lived, I was so grateful to be there. The flat was perfect and I quickly settled in.

My new address was also police marked. Fitted with a 'blue box' which was connected directly to the police. If I was in danger and pressed the blue box, the police would receive an instant alert and be at my door immediately.

Meanwhile I applied for Clare's law. The law I learned about during my stay at the mental health crisis centre. 'Clare's Law' allows you to request information about your partner's past history of domestic violence or abusive behaviour.

Before facing Chris in the courtroom, I needed to be certain whether I had truly been the cause of his anger, as he had claimed. I simply couldn't bring myself to send a man to prison if it turned out to be my fault.

When the report came back, I learned that I was his 7th victim on record. He was very dangerous and violent, a serial abuser who had already been to prison for assaulting another woman.

I Googled his name and discovered that he had been wanted by police in another county a few years earlier for failing to attend court for GBH charges. This news cleared my mind of blame and gave me the final strength I needed to face him in court.

It took two months for Chris to be tracked down and arrested. Late one evening, I received a call from the police, informing me that Chris had finally been arrested and was now in custody.

When questioned, Chris denied carrying out any assaults on me. This surprisingly shocked me. Nevertheless, they had enough evidence for the CPS to charge him.

Once arrested, he played the legal system by pleading not guilty at every court date to delay and avoid conviction. He was approved for bail and tagged until the trial date.

During the two-year wait for my court date, I saw many other cases related to violence against women on the news, like Sarah Everard, Patrycja Wyrebek, Susan Baird, Alyson Nelson and Sabina Nessa. Their stories were chilling, making me realise how lucky I was to have escaped a similar fate.

During the 2 year wait for the trial I was told I cannot start trauma therapy until after the trial because Chris's defence lawyer could argue in court that the memories I recalled were distorted by the treatment.

The plan was to keep me medicated, avoid triggers, and call 999 if I reached a crisis point. I would start my EMDR trauma treatment after the trial.

As the months dragged on, I didn't think it could but my PTSD was getting noticeably worse. I had a couple more mental health crises resulting in admissions to the crisis house.

By this time, I had gained over 4 stone in weight and was stuttering constantly from anxiety. I was on high alert all the time, couldn't go outside, overcome with crying spells, nightmares and regular deep depression. I just wasn't coping and for once in my life I didn't know how to fix it.

Knowing I wouldn't be able to start treatment until after the trial and with no support or intermediate step between medication and a full-blown mental health breakdown,

The mental health crisis team assigned me a mental health peer worker from an NHS charity called **VoiceAbility**. My peer worker would visit my home once a week to accompany me on walks outside, which proved to be a lifeline.

During one of my better days I saw my next-door neighbour outside our house. I introduce myself, and she suggested I should pop in for a drink once lockdown is lifted and the covid days are behind us. It was refreshing to have such a nice neighbour after everything I experienced in my last neighbourhood.

Lock down continued and my neighbour started inviting me for walks to get me out of the house. It was as if she understood that I was going through a tough time, and that it was more than just lockdown boredom. I ended up confiding in her about what I was dealing with she was so understanding and supportive.

Our walks became a weekly routine where we would walk Dylan around Regents Park. It was a relief to have such a kind neighbour.

My local pub friend Terry would also regularly check in on me and go for walks.

After two postponements, my court date finally arrived in April 2022. On the morning of my trial, I received a surprising call from the Crown Prosecution lawyer informing me that Chris was offering to plead guilty to two of the most serious charges if the third assault charge was dropped. If I agreed to this deal, I would not have to take the stand or even go to court. He would be automatically sentenced on the 2 charges.

Without hesitation, I declined outright. I told them I would rather take the stand and have him be found not guilty than agree to drop one of the charges. Accepting the deal would essentially mean acknowledging that the third assault never happened, and I couldn't agree to that. It didn't sit right with me, and I wasn't afraid of standing up in court or being cross-examined.

When I arrived at court, Chris pleaded guilty to all three assault charges as soon as he was told I was there in person. It was clear he didn't want me to take the stand. I then entered the courtroom to witness his guilty plea and personally read my victim impact statement. Chris, who came up from the cells because he had broken his bail conditions stood right in front of me in the glass dock as I addressed the court. When I finished reading my statement the judge asked when I would be starting my treatment, and I told him I would follow up that day. He wished me well and dismissed me from the stand, and I left the courtroom.

Chris was sentenced to 50 months in prison. The first thing I did when I got home was call the Doctors to finally get my EDMR trauma therapy started.

Justice is supposed to mean fairness and moral rightness. But as I would come to learn in the months ahead, true justice is more complicated than simply winning a court case. Abusers often receive shockingly short sentences compared to the life sentence of pain inflicted on their victims.

The reality is the trauma doesn't end when the gavel strikes on a guilty verdict. In many ways, that's only the beginning.

# CHAPTER 9: THE LONG ROAD TO RECOVERY

I have fully settled into my home and community. It's been six years since I was first diagnosed with PTSD, 3 years with C-PTSD, four years since the final assault, and two years since the trial. I am constantly aware that I am lucky to be alive after surviving such brutal attacks.

Asides from the police that dealt with my case and my mental health team I have been let down by every support system I've been placed in. Sadly I regularly find myself fighting just to get basic support from local authorities and government agencies and often feel the underlying stigma that still exists around mental health issues in society.

Twelve months after my trial, I was still on the lengthy NHS waiting list to receive EMDR trauma treatment. It turned out NHS iCope mixed up my records with another patient, referring me for incorrect therapy and later forgetting about me until I followed up.

After a good conversation with my HR Director and Manager, who was incredibly supportive, guided me to seek private treatment through my workplace Bupa policy. Finally I started my treatment in March 2023. For the past 18 months, I have been receiving weekly EMDR trauma treatments.

I was offered the option of restorative justice where I could potentially meet with Chris under supervision but I declined.

I didn't need to see him for closure. I took the time to educate myself about his creed, which helped me reconcile my thoughts and feelings about him and the crimes he committed against me.

Twelve months after the trial, I received a call from the parole board informing me that Chris was potentially being released early from prison due to good behaviour. He had served just 16 months of a 50 month sentence.

To date, I am on a lot of medication. I am now registered as disabled. I have endured six mental health crises and received diagnoses of severe clinical C-PTSD. I have little to no memory of my crisis episodes and  it takes me weeks sometimes months to climb out of them.

I am experiencing a delay between my thoughts and speech therefore I am currently being investigated for a traumatic brain injury (TBI) caused by asphyxiation and repeated head trauma.

The C-PTSD has continued to dominate and affect every domain of my life. I struggle to breathe with 2-3 anxiety attacks every day. I suffer from regular agoraphobia, night terrors, sleep paralysis, dissociation, crippling depression, and chronic nerve pain on the side of my face and body.

My constant hypervigilance is exhausting. I rarely go out, and when I do,  it's only during daylight to familiar places, along a familiar route, and only with people I know and trust. Every step is carefully thought through. I can't talk to strangers, avoid all public social media, and refuse to allow photos of me to be posted online that disclose my real-time location. When I'm in a public room, I need to sit with my back to the wall facing my eyes on the exit.

I only told my immediate family - my mother and brothers - about what had happened to me just three weeks before my trial. I put off telling them but in the end it was obvious something was wrong with me so I told them.

During better periods, I take the opportunity to visit home in Wales and spend time walking the familiar streets and mountains, and meeting up with childhood friends. This I find very grounding. They knew me long before the abuse, and it helps me reconnect with myself and who I was before the trauma.

In my own time I told a few close friends about what happened to me, and they have been shocked and heartbroken. Lately, it hasn't been as easy to go home, as more people have noticed the decline in my health, and I'm being asked about it more directly.

As part of processing everything, I began writing down what had happened to me as a form of therapy, helping me organise my thoughts and feelings in an effort to move forward.

Along the way, both male and female victims have privately opened up to me, making me realise just how many perpetrators of abuse get away with destroying lives.

This makes me think further about how many victims have been silenced by the mental manipulation of their abuser.

The pattern is always familiar—they silence their victims with shame while wearing them down through the "wheel of abuse." Down the line leaving their victims carrying the can, turning to drugs, alcohol or even suicide because they just cant cope with the trauma.

This experience also opened my eyes to the lack of support and the organisations that fail to follow their own protocols, leaving vulnerable victims lost in the system. It can happen to anyone. Abuse doesn't discriminate.

If I could give advice to anyone currently enduring an abusive relationship, I would urge them to seek out the correct information from domestic abuse professionals that can help you to safely leave the relationship. **The wheel of abuse keeps victims trapped** - learn about it and how to recognise it, break the cycle, and leave.

Friends and family who want to help someone they care about in an abusive situation should also educate themselves on the dynamics of domestic abuse. You too can reach out to an expert for guidance on how to approach your loved one when you suspect they are being mentally, financially or physically abused.

I'd also urge any victim, as well as their loved ones, to learn about **Clare's Law** and file for it to get the full picture of what the police already know. This information is confidential and could **save your life.**

Government authorities, local councillors, Adult Services, the DWP, CICA, and local councils must do better in supporting victims of these devastating crimes. The often gruelling processes and lack of adequate support not only exacerbates the trauma but also makes the path to recovery significantly more difficult—sometimes even impossible.

Employers also have a responsibility to educate themselves on domestic violence, abuse, coercive control, and the impact of PTSD and complex PTSD on an individual's ability to work. It's crucial that they understand how to provide appropriate support and implement safeguarding measures for employees who may be victims and suffering in silence.

Everyone should be aware of the company's call to action when identifying the signs. At the time I had an **incredibly supportive manager, and HR team** which at times was all I had.

Finally, I'd urge any abuser to seek help immediately before their actions escalate to the point of destroying lives and landing them in prison.

I want to thank my family and friends, here in London, Miami and back home in Wales, for their love, care, patience and understanding.

My mental health team, my work colleagues and boss for their ongoing help and support.

A special mention goes to Michael Brown, founder of Clare's Law, in loving memory of his daughter Clare Wood.

Lastly, thanks to my neighbours, my friend Terry, and of course, my dog Dylan.

All of these people some without evening knowing helped me at a time when I could't help myself, and for that I will always be forever grateful.

Ria.

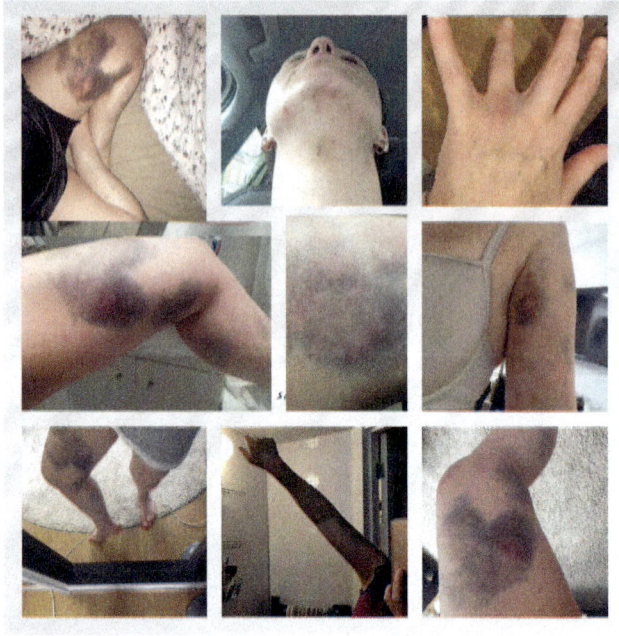
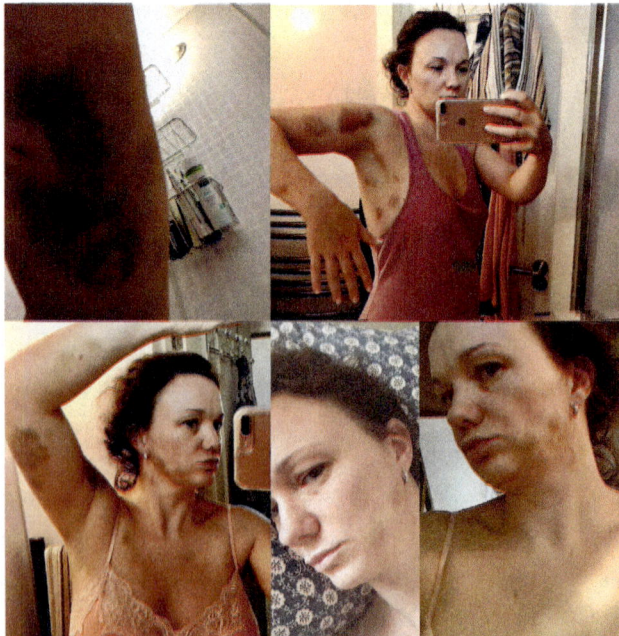

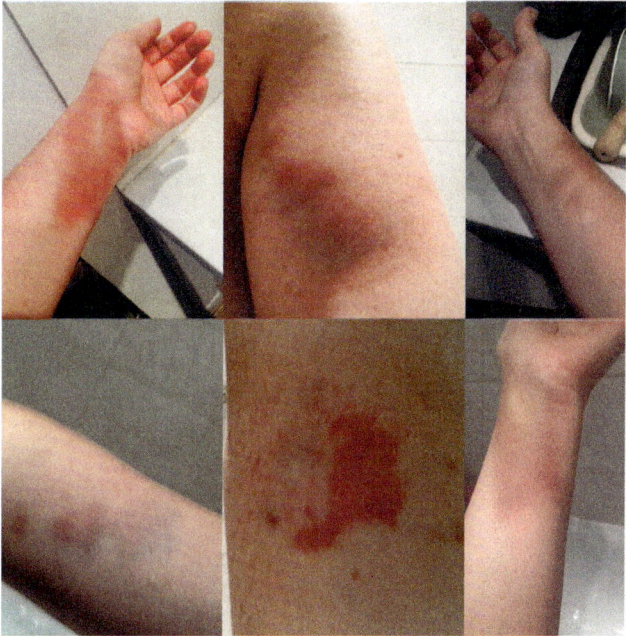

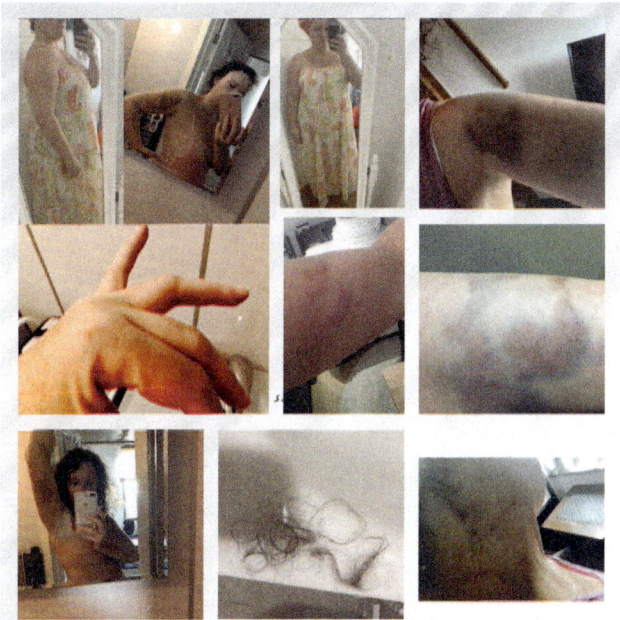

# VICTIM IMPACT STATEMENT

R ia Davies Victim Impact Statement.

## April 2022

For 20 years, I have travelled the world working in the cruise industry. The later years I was promoted to the corporate office in Miami where I lived. I was a very independent woman, well known in my industry. I enjoyed life, and meeting new people.  I throughly enjoyed my career, and working hard. I was known for keeping in touch with friends around the world I meet on my travels.

In 2017 I relocated to London and I was looking forwards to the new chapter in my life working at L'Oréal UKi. I reconnected with Chris and this is when behind closed doors my life changed.

The trauma from the abuse I have encountered at the hands of Chris is overwhelming and have changed my life.
In result I have been diagnosed with C-PDST.  From the time I wake up until the time I go to bed my mind and body is on high alert.
I am constantly anxious, scared, and nervous to leave the house. In result I hardly leave my home.

I have had several mental health crisis. On 3 occasions I was admitted into the mental health crisis house in London. I have Night terrors of Chris and the violent assaults he put me through. Most went on for hours, some for days.

In result I have depression, I cry allot, I stutter, lost all my confidence, I don't trust anyone, I never feel safe, I spend all my time alone, and often experience suicidal thoughts.

A few occasions when I just couldn't cope anymore, I came very close to taking my life.

My prescribed medication makes me sleepy but this dose is necessary to keep me safe and get me through my day. I have missed months of work due to my mental health being so bad..

I don't want to see anyone, I avoid leaving my house. I lost all interest in hobbies and pass times. In result has effected my relationships with friends, co workers and family. I feel nobody understands my mental suffering, and I feel isolated from the world. I have overwhelming sadness, and shame of the abuse I suffered at the hands of Chris.

My warm feelings for Chris were genuine. I have always had a strong will to never give up on people, always give people a chance and the benefit of the doubt. This outlook has made me very successful in life. However, this strength became my weakness when I meet Chris. He used my values to his advantage and manipulated me, wore me down with mentally abuse and violent assaults.

Because of the embarrassment and shame of the abuse. I tried to hide from my family and friends what was going on behind closed doors. It simply became easier to take a beating from Chris, than tell anyone and explain how I got to this point, let alone them understanding. I was so worn down I didn't even understand what was happening myself.

I covered my bruises to go to work, I made up stories to explain my injuries. I carried on as normal until eventually my mental health and nerves from the abuse consumed me and I landed up in a mental health crisis facility. After the last assault on 23rd July 2020, I went to A&E and finally had the strength to come forwards and reported Chris to the police.

Chris has no respect for the law, It took months for the police to track him down. Chris plays the legal system and has no remorse to what he's done to me and how it has affected my life. Chris has not admitted to what he has done to me, instead HE has dragged me through a 2 year court procedure which has lead us up to, today's trial. During this time my EMDR trauma treatment for C-PDST has had to be placed on hold until after this trial.

I am worried about my future, I suffer when I'm awake and when I'm asleep. I get mentally exhausted. I am so ashamed of what Chris has done to me. I often feel defeated and can't see any light at the end of the tunnel. This leads me back my to depression, crippling anxiety, and suicidal thoughts. It's a never ending vicious circle.

Overall this has made my world very small.
I am trying everyday, but I'm not the same person.

Chris is a very dangerous, violent man and needs to be rehabilitated before he damages other people's lives, like he has mine. I wish him well on his journey.

Ria Davies.

Printed in Great Britain
by Amazon